SUPER CUTE!
Baby Horses

by Bethany Olson

DELPHI PUBLIC LIBRARY
222 East Main Street
Delphi, Indiana 46923
765-564-2929

BELLWETHER MEDIA

Note to Librarians, Teachers, and Parents:

Blastoff! Readers are carefully developed by literacy experts and combine standards-based content with developmentally appropriate text.

Level 1 provides the most support through repetition of high-frequency words, light text, predictable sentence patterns, and strong visual support.

Level 2 offers early readers a bit more challenge through varied simple sentences, increased text load, and less repetition of high-frequency words.

Level 3 advances early-fluent readers toward fluency through increased text and concept load, less reliance on visuals, longer sentences, and more literary language.

Level 4 builds reading stamina by providing more text per page, increased use of punctuation, greater variation in sentence patterns, and increasingly challenging vocabulary.

Level 5 encourages children to move from "learning to read" to "reading to learn" by providing even more text, varied writing styles, and less familiar topics.

Whichever book is right for your reader, Blastoff! Readers are the perfect books to build confidence and encourage a love of reading that will last a lifetime!

This edition first published in 2014 by Bellwether Media, Inc.

No part of this publication may be reproduced in whole or in part without written permission of the publisher. For information regarding permission, write to Bellwether Media, Inc., Attention: Permissions Department, 5357 Penn Avenue South, Minneapolis, MN 55419.

Library of Congress Cataloging-in-Publication Data

Olson, Bethany.
 Baby horses / by Bethany Olson.
   p. cm. – (Blastoff! readers. Super cute!)
 Audience: K to grade 3.
 Summary: "Developed by literacy experts for students in kindergarten through grade three, this book introduces baby horses to young readers through leveled text and related photos"– Provided by publisher.
 Includes bibliographical references and index.
 ISBN 978-1-60014-928-3 (hardcover : alk. paper)
 1. Foals–Juvenile literature. 2. Horses–Juvenile literature. 3. Animals–Infancy–Juvenile literature. I. Title.
 SF302.O575 2014
 636.1'07–dc23
                                                                    2013007819

Text copyright © 2014 by Bellwether Media, Inc. BLASTOFF! READERS and associated logos are trademarks and/or registered trademarks of Bellwether Media, Inc. SCHOLASTIC, CHILDREN'S PRESS, and associated logos are trademarks and/or registered trademarks of Scholastic Inc.

Printed in the United States of America, North Mankato, MN.

Table of Contents

Foals!	4
On Its Feet	8
Growing Up	16
Glossary	22
To Learn More	23
Index	24

Foals!

Baby horses are called foals. They live on farms.

Foals grow up to be large horses or small ponies.

On Its Feet

A foal is born with long legs. It stands up soon after birth.

A foal **trots** the day it is born. It **gallops** the next day.

The foal needs naps. Hay or grass makes a soft bed.

Mom **nuzzles** her foal to show love.

Growing Up

Young foals need mom for food. They drink her milk.

Older foals eat hay, grains, and other **solid food**.

Foals become **yearlings** on their first birthday. They are big now!

Glossary

gallops—runs fast with all four feet in the air at the same time

nuzzles—rubs with the nose and mouth

solid food—food other than milk; solid food for horses is hay and grains.

trots—moves faster than walking speed

yearlings—horses that are one year old

To Learn More

AT THE LIBRARY

Editors of Kingfisher. *Baby Animals On the Farm.* New York, N.Y.: Kingfisher, 2010.

Elora, Grace. *Foals.* New York, N.Y.: Gareth Stevens Pub., 2011.

Kalman, Bobbie. *Baby Horses.* New York, N.Y.: Crabtree Pub., 2008.

ON THE WEB

Learning more about horses is as easy as 1, 2, 3.

1. Go to www.factsurfer.com.

2. Enter "horses" into the search box.

3. Click the "Surf" button and you will see a list of related Web sites.

With factsurfer.com, finding more information is just a click away.

Index

bed, 12
birthday, 20
born, 8, 10
drink, 16
eat, 18
farms, 4
food, 16
gallops, 10
grains, 18
grass, 12
grow, 6
hay, 12, 18
horses, 6
legs, 8
love, 14
milk, 16
mom, 14, 16

naps, 12
nuzzles, 14
ponies, 6
solid food, 18
stands, 8
trots, 10
yearlings, 20

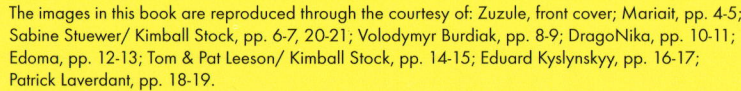